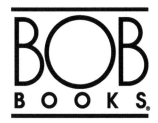

Reading Adventures!

ISBN 978-0-545-62285-1

The New Puppy (ISBN 978-0-545-38268-7) © 2012 by Lynn Maslen Kertell.
Cupcake Surprise (ISBN 978-0-545-38269-4) © 2012 by Lynn Maslen Kertell.
My School Trip (ISBN 978-0-545-38270-0) © 2012 by Lynn Maslen Kertell.
Outdoor Adventures! (ISBN 978-0-545-38271-7) © 2012 by Lynn Maslen Kertell.
Buddy to the Rescue (ISBN 978-0-545-38273-1) © 2012 by Lynn Maslen Kertell.
I Can Ride! (ISBN 978-0-545-38272-4) © 2012 by Lynn Maslen Kertell.

12 11 10 9 8 7 6 5 4 3 2 1   13 14 15 16 17 18/0

Printed in Singapore   46
This edition first printing, June 2013

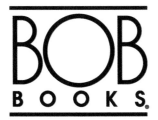

Reading Adventures!

by Lynn Maslen Kertell
illustrated by Sue Hendra

SCHOLASTIC INC.

Table of Contents

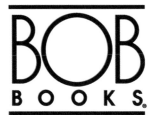

The New Puppy

by Lynn Maslen Kertell
illustrated by Sue Hendra

SCHOLASTIC INC.

Jack and Anna want a puppy.

A puppy is a friend.

A puppy likes to play.

"A puppy is a lot of work,"
say Mom and Dad.

"Puppies need to be fed," says Dad.

"Puppies need to go out," says Mom.

"We will take care of it," the kids say.

Jack and Anna can do a
good job.

There are many dogs at the
pet shelter.

Big dogs, small dogs,
fluffy dogs, shaggy dogs.

Jack and Anna like
the brown puppy.

The puppy gives Anna a kiss.

"What will you name your pet?" asks Mom.

"We can call him Buddy!"
says Jack.

Buddy loves to chase a ball.

He loves to tug a rope.

Jack and Anna want to draw.

Buddy wants to help.

Jack and Anna make a fort.

Buddy jumps in.

"Time to go out," says Mom.

Buddy runs and runs.

Anna gives Buddy his dinner.

Jack gives him water.

Buddy is tired.

Buddy falls fast asleep.

Tomorrow, Buddy will be ready
to play again.

Cupcake Surprise!

by LYNN MASLEN KERTELL
illustrated by SUE HENDRA

SCHOLASTIC INC.

It is Dad's birthday.

What will Jack and Anna
give to Dad?

Will they make a card?
Will they jot a note?
Will they sing a song?

Jack and Anna will
make cupcakes for Dad.

Cupcakes will be a big surprise.

Anna has the cookbook.

Jack gets eggs, sugar, and milk.

Oh, no. There is no flour.

That is not a good surprise.

Jack and Anna go to the store.

At the store they get flour.
They get cookies, too.

Jack puts in flour and sugar.
Anna puts in milk, butter, and eggs.

Stir it up, Jack!

Uh-oh! The cookies fall in.
That is a surprise.

They mix in the cookies.

Oh, no! Chips fall in.
That is a surprise.

They mix in the chips.

Stir it all up, Jack.

Buddy wants to help, too.

Mom puts the cupcakes in to bake.

Jack and Anna watch the cupcakes.
Buddy watches, too.

The cupcakes look good.

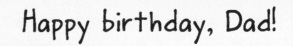

Happy birthday, Dad!

Here are your birthday cupcakes.

Surprise!
These cupcakes taste great!

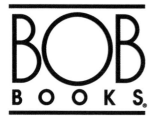

SCHOLASTIC READER
LEVEL 1
50-250 WORDS

My School Trip

by LYNN MASLEN KERTELL
illustrated by SUE HENDRA

SCHOLASTIC INC.

Jack's class is going on a trip.

They will take a bus to the zoo.

Jack sits with Bill.

The zoo is full of things to see.
Jack hears the chatter of animal
sounds.

Bill sniffs new smells.

Jack and Bill see zebras and giraffes.

Next, Jack and Bill see goats.

71

That sound came from a tiger.

Jack hears the tiger roar another loud roar.

Next, the class sees polar bears.

Bill hears a new sound. "*Hoot, hoot, hoot.*"
It is not an owl. What can it be?

75

"Monkeys!" yells Bill.

"I can't hear you," shouts Jack.

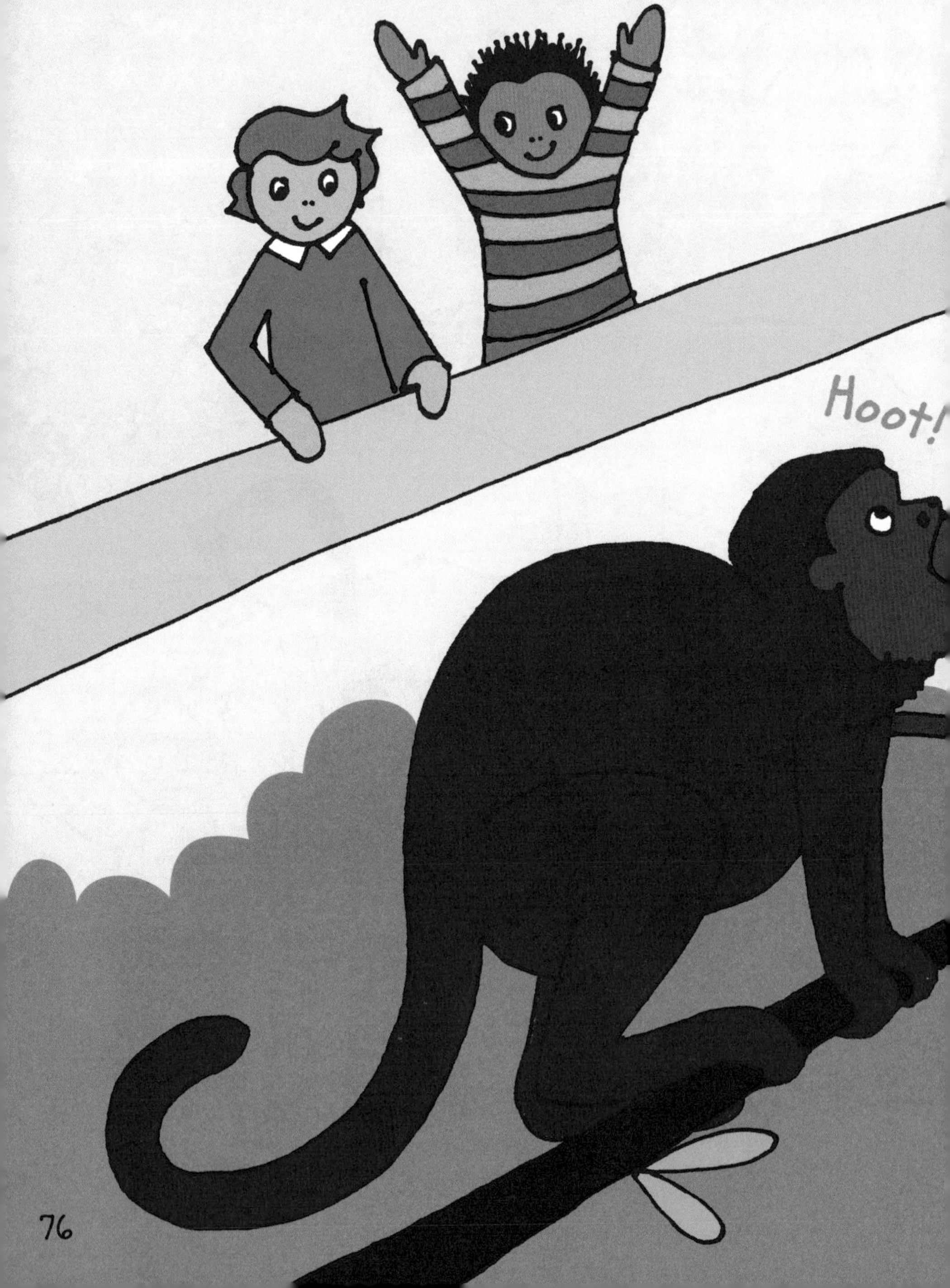

The monkeys hoot, howl, and yelp.
They are very loud.

Hoot!

Bill wants to follow his nose.

But Jack can hear screeching around the corner.

Screech, Screech!

Jack can feed the birds.

Jack's class sits down for lunch.
They listen to the sounds of the zoo.

They hear a shout. *"Hello! Hello!"*
A peacock yells its greeting from the
roof.

Hello!

Hello!

The peacock wants lunch.
A man from the zoo feeds the bird.

Jack and Bill find a gift from the peacock.

The kids hear another sound.
"Ha, ha, ha!" What makes that sound?

Is it a frog? Is it a wild dog?
Is it a bird?

Ha, ha ha!

Ha, ha ha!

It is children yelling!

Jack's class joins in and makes the sounds of the zoo.
They roar, hoot, screech, and yell!

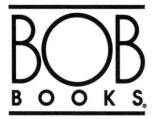

SCHOLASTIC READER
LEVEL 1
50-250 WORDS

Outdoor Adventures!

by LYNN MASLEN KERTELL
illustrated by SUE HENDRA

SCHOLASTIC INC.

"Jack, Jack, Dad will take us on a hike today!" yells Anna.

Anna puts on sunscreen.
Jack runs to the car.

Dad brings lunch and drinks.

Jack and Anna sit in the car.
They ride and ride.

They pass the city.
They drive to the country.

"We are here!" says Dad.

Jack and Anna start up the path.

They go under trees.
They cross a stream.

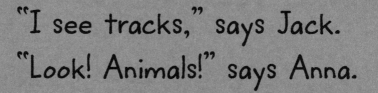

"I see tracks," says Jack.
"Look! Animals!" says Anna.

103

Dad puts the picnic blanket
on the grass.
"Give that back," says Jack
to the frisky squirrel.

The sun is low.
The air cools down.
It is time to go home.

"I love hiking with you, Dad," says Anna.

"Thanks, Dad!" says Jack
as he gives Dad a hug.

The next day, Jack and Anna
want to go on another hike.

They make a picnic.
They get ready.

Mom says, "Not today, kids."

"Today you can not
go on a hike."

Jack and Anna do not drive in the car.

They do not pass the city.

They do not go into the country.

Jack says, "I know
what we can do."

Jack and Anna go in the yard.

Jack and Anna walk up the path.

They go under trees.
They cross a stream.

"Look! Animals!" says Anna.

Anna puts their picnic
blanket on the grass.

"Give that back!" says Jack
to the frisky puppy.

The sun gets low.
The air cools down.

"Come in," calls Mom.

"We made our own hike,"
say Jack and Anna.
"Yes, you did,"
agree Mom and Dad.

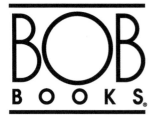

SCHOLASTIC READER
LEVEL 1
50-250 WORDS

Buddy to
the Rescue

by LYNN MASLEN KERTELL
illustrated by SUE HENDRA

SCHOLASTIC INC.

"Do you hear that?" says Anna.

Jack and Anna run out the door.

They hear horns. They hear drums.
A fair has come to town.

"Let's get Buddy and go!" says Anna.

Anna and Jack and Mom and Dad
walk to the fair.

Mom gets tickets.
Jack goes on a ride.

"Dad, I want to play a game,"
says Anna.
Dad plays the game, too.

"Ruff, ruff," says Buddy.

"Buddy, you can not have a hot dog," says Anna.

135

Buddy looks big.
Buddy looks small.
Buddy looks like a funny dog.

"Let's go on the bumper cars," says Anna.

Boom! Bang!
Anna and Jack crack and crash
their cars.

"*Ruff, ruff,*" says Buddy.

"Buddy, no! You can not have a
hot dog," says Anna.

Buddy barks.

Buddy runs to the hot dog stand.

Anna sees smoke.
Anna sees fire.

"Dad! Dad!" shouts Anna.

Sound the alarm. Ring the bell.

Call 911.
There is a fire at the
hot dog stand!

The fire truck is on its way.
The siren is very loud.
Red lights flash.

The fire truck pulls up.

Water sprays. Smoke puffs.

Buddy is safe. The fire is out.
The hot dog man is safe, too.

Buddy is a hero.
Buddy saw the fire first.

Anna gives Buddy a hug.

The firemen pat Buddy.

"Buddy, now you can have your hot dog," says Anna.

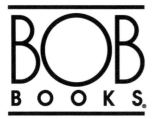

BOB
BOOKS.

SCHOLASTIC READER
LEVEL 1
50-250 WORDS

I Can Ride!

by LYNN MASLEN KERTELL
illustrated by SUE HENDRA

SCHOLASTIC INC.

It is a beautiful day.
"We can all go on a bike ride,"
says Dad.

Anna is a good bike rider.

She pedals at the park.

She goes up and down hills.

Dad says, "Jack, you can go with me."

163

"I want to ride on two wheels," says Jack.

"Okay, we can try,"
says Dad.

Dad gets his tools.

Dad takes the little wheels
off Jack's bike.

The bike is hard to ride.
The bike wobbles.

The bike falls.
Jack can not ride the bike.

Dad says, "Jack, I will help you."
Dad takes Jack to a big lot.

The land is smooth and flat.
The ground is black and hard.

Dad holds on to the back of the bike.

The bike wobbles.
The bike skids.

Jack is scared.

Dad says, "Do not give up, Jack.
We can try at the park."

Dad and Jack go up a small hill.
Dad says, "You can do it, Jack."

Jack sits on the bike.
He puts his feet on the ground.
Then he lifts his feet.

The bike does not wobble.
The bike does not tip.
Jack glides down the small hill.

"Dad, I did it!
I want to do it again!"

Jack rolls down the hill again and again and again.

Next, Jack puts his feet
on the pedals.

His feet push.
The pedals spin.
The bike goes and goes.

"Dad! I did it!" shouts Jack.

Jack rides in the park.
He goes around a bend.

He stops. He starts.
Jack is a bike rider!

Jack calls Grandma. He tells her the good news.

Grandma has a surprise for Jack.

"Now you are a bike rider.
We can all go together!"
says Grandma.

"Yippee!" yells Jack as he pedals away.

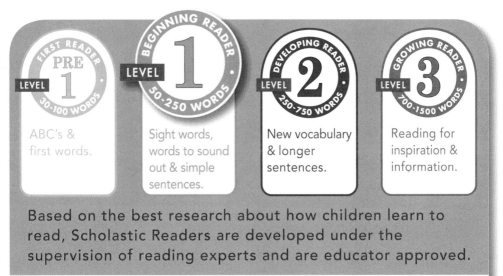

FIRST READER
PRE
LEVEL 1
30-100 WORDS
ABC's & first words.

BEGINNING READER
LEVEL 1
50-250 WORDS
Sight words, words to sound out & simple sentences.

DEVELOPING READER
LEVEL 2
250-750 WORDS
New vocabulary & longer sentences.

GROWING READER
LEVEL 3
700-1500 WORDS
Reading for inspiration & information.

Based on the best research about how children learn to read, Scholastic Readers are developed under the supervision of reading experts and are educator approved.

BEGINNING READER	GRADE LEVEL	GUIDED READING LEVEL	LEXILE® LEVEL	WORD COUNT
Level 1	Pre-K–1	G-H	60L-330L	158-236